Magic Ballerina

Delphie and the Fairy Godmother

Welcome to the world of Enchantia!

I have always loved to dance. The captivating music and wonderful stories of ballet are so inspiring. So come with me and let's follow Delphie on her magical adventures in Enchantia, where the stories of dance will take you on a very special journey.

(signature)

p.s. Turn to the back to learn a special dance step from me...

Special thanks to
Linda Chapman and
Katie May

First published in Great Britain by HarperCollins *Children's Books* 2008
HarperCollins *Children's Books* is a division of HarperCollins *Publishers* Ltd,
77-85 Fulham Palace Road, Hammersmith, London W6 8JB

The HarperCollins *Children's Books* website address is
www.harpercollins.co.uk

1

Text copyright © HarperCollins *Children's Books* 2008
Illustrations by Katie May
Illustrations copyright © HarperCollins *Children's Books* 2008

ISBN 978 0 00 785913 9

Printed and bound in England by
Clays Ltd, St Ives plc

Magic Ballerina™

Delphie and the Fairy Godmother

Darcey Bussell

HarperCollins *Children's Books*

To Phoebe and Zoe, as they are the inspiration behind Magic Ballerina.

Contents

Prologue

In the soft, pale light, the girl stood
with her head bent and her hands
held lightly in front of her.
There was a moment's silence and then
the first notes of the music began.
For as long as the girl could remember
music had seemed to tell her of
another world – a magical, exciting
world – that lay far, far away.
She always felt if she could just
close her eyes and lose herself,
then she would get there.
Maybe this time. As the music
swirled inside her, she swept
her arms above her head, rose on to
her toes and began to dance…

The New Girl

Delphie ran up the stone steps of the ballet school, excitement bubbling through her. It would soon be time for her ballet class. As she reached the big wooden door, she thought back to a time six months ago when she had walked past the building every day, wishing she could have lessons there. It had been like a dream come true when the teacher, Madame Za-Za, had seen her watching from outside the school one afternoon and offered to teach her for free. Delphie had learned so much since then – and had so much fun. She had performed on stage and, even better than that, she had been to Enchantia!

Delphie smiled to herself as she thought about the secret land. An old pair of red ballet shoes used magic to whisk her away there and whenever she went she ended up having an amazing adventure with her new friends.

I wonder when I'll go to Enchantia again, Delphie thought, shutting the door behind her and running down the corridor to the changing rooms. She always liked to get to

class early so she could practise before any
of her classmates arrived.

As Delphie pushed back the door she
saw a girl, just a bit younger than her,
sitting on a bench in the changing rooms.
She was pretty with big blue eyes and wavy
blonde hair pulled back into a bun. Delphie's
heart sank. It was the new girl, Rosa.

She had started at Madame Za-Za's ballet
school a week ago. Delphie had tried
talking to her a few times but Rosa just
ignored her or answered questions with a
brief "yes" or "no".

As Delphie walked across the changing
room, Rosa looked down, not saying
anything.

"Hi," Delphie said, trying to be friendly
but Rosa didn't reply.

Delphie started to take off her school
uniform but it was strange getting changed
in silence. Usually the girls all chatted
together. "You're here early," she tried again.

Rosa nodded but just continued tying the
ribbons on her ballet shoes without
speaking.

There was a pause so Delphie tried again. "Did you dance a lot before you started classes here?"

"A bit," Rosa said briefly.

At least it was a reply. Delphie felt encouraged. She usually got on with most people so she didn't like feeling uncomfortable with Rosa. "You're really good at *petit jetés*," she said admiringly. "I was behind you in the last class. I wish I could do them as well as you."

Delphie thought Rosa wasn't going to say anything in return but then the new girl took a deep breath. "Yes. I've always found them easy. You find them hard, don't you? I noticed in class. I…"

Delphie was stung. "I don't find them *that* difficult!"

Rosa suddenly jumped up and hurried out of the room.

Delphie stared after her crossly. The cheek of it! She'd been trying to be friendly! There'd been no need for Rosa to say she wasn't good at something. Maybe she did find the small jumps springing from one foot to the other quite hard, but she could do lots of other dance steps OK. Rosa could have commented on those things instead!

Feeling fed up, Delphie finished getting changed. Once she was dressed she tied her

long dark hair back and headed out to the ballet studio.

Rosa was in there practising a *pas de chat*. Delphie paused by the door. She loved the light sideways leap. You had to keep your knees out to the side, but Rosa was having problems and Delphie could immediately see why.

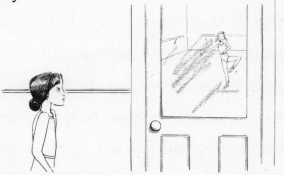

She's springing off her front foot, she thought. Part of Delphie wanted to go straight in and help Rosa but at the back of her mind a small voice was saying, *Why should you? She's really unfriendly.*

So Delphie decided not to help. The other dance studio was still empty; she'd go and warm up in there instead. As she turned away, she started in surprise. Madame Za-Za was watching her from the doorway of her office just down the corridor.

"Madame Za-Za!" Delphie said.

Madame Za-Za's expression cleared. "Hello, Delphie," she said, walking towards her. "How are you?"

"Fine, thank you." Delphie felt a bit embarrassed.

"Are you going into warm-up with Rosa before class?" her teacher went on.

Delphie's cheeks reddened slightly. "I... I thought I might go in the other dance studio."

"Oh." For a moment Madame Za-Za didn't say anything but then she glanced at Delphie. "Everyone deserves a chance, Delphie," she said quietly. "I would have thought you would have realised that."

Delphie stared. It was as if Madame Za-Za had read her mind, seen her thoughts about Rosa and not wanting to help her. "But... I..."

"I'll see you in class in ten minutes," Madame Za-Za said as she turned to go back to her office.

Delphie walked slowly into the other dance studio, thinking about the look on Madame Za-Za's face. Did she think Delphie was being horrible? She hated the thought that she had disappointed her dance teacher in some way, but she felt too awkward now to go in and talk to Rosa. Trying not to dwell on what had just happened, Delphie went to the *barre*, moved her feet into second position and

began to slowly bend and
straighten her knees.

When her class
finally started she
kept watching
Rosa. She knew her
best friends, Poppy and
Lola, thought the new girl
was just shy.

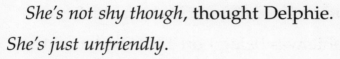

She's not shy though, thought Delphie.
She's just unfriendly.

But when Delphie went to bed that night
she was still thinking about it and she
couldn't get the disappointed expression on
Madame Za-Za's face out of her mind.
Maybe she *should* give Rosa more of a
chance.

I'll see what she's like tomorrow, Delphie decided.

When Delphie arrived at the ballet school the next day, Rosa was already in the studio practising *pas de chats*, and she was still having problems. Delphie hesitated. What should she do?

Suddenly her feet began to tingle. She looked down. Her red ballet shoes were glowing! She was about to go to Enchantia!

A Thorny Problem

A rainbow of swirling colours surrounded
Delphie and swept her away. Round and
round she spun, up in the air until she was
set down on to firm ground and the colours
faded.

As Delphie looked around her she saw
she was standing in front of a massive
thicket of trees and thorny brambles. There

were no houses or people. How strange.
The shoes usually brought her to Enchantia
when there was a problem to solve but she
couldn't see how she was needed this time.

"Hello!" she called.

No one answered so she began to walk
into the trees. The thorns caught at her
clothes and she tripped over tree roots on
the ground. It was strangely quiet in the
forest. No birds were singing and there
were no animals to be seen.

Delphie pushed on until she reached a
wall of brambles so thick that there was no
way through. She sank down on to a tree
stump in frustration. What was she going
to do now?

Then, suddenly, there was a tinkling

noise behind her. Delphie looked round
and saw a beautiful ballerina appear in a
shimmering haze. Dressed in a lilac tutu
with a sparkling bodice, her brown hair
was caught up in a
diamond tiara.
The ballerina's
arms were held
high above her
head and she
was carrying a
wand in her
right hand. The
wings on her
back were almost

see-through and glinted with faint rainbow
colours. But they weren't pretend wings

like on a costume, Delphie realised. They
were real!

"Delphie!" the fairy cried. "I'm so glad
you've come!"

"Hi. Who are you?" Delphie couldn't
help smiling at her.

"I'm the Lilac Fairy from *Sleeping Beauty*.
Lila for short," the fairy answered. "I'm one
of Princess Aurelia's fairy godmothers. I've
heard all about you from Aurelia and the
Sugar Plum Fairy. Oh, Delphie, we're in
real trouble," she cried. "The Royal Palace
has been covered with thorns and is now
hidden behind these brambles. Everyone in
the palace is asleep including Aurelia. She'll
only wake up when a prince – her one true
love – kisses her."

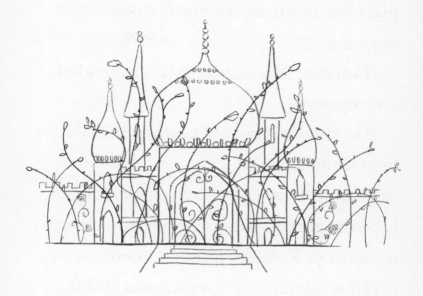

"Of course," Delphie breathed,
remembering the story of *Sleeping Beauty*.

Lila went on. "At Aurelia's christening,
the King and Queen forgot to invite the
Wicked Fairy, but she came anyway and
put a curse on Princess Aurelia that meant
that on her eighteenth birthday she would

prick her finger on the spindle of a spinning wheel and sleep for a hundred years." Lila shuddered. "I wasn't able to stop the curse completely but my magic was able to change it so that if Aurelia did prick her finger she would still fall asleep but would wake when her prince kissed her. And now that day has happened and it's all King Rat's fault!"

"King Rat!" Delphie exclaimed. She should have known. King Rat was horrible. He hated dancing and was always trying to stop everyone from having fun. Every time she had been in Enchantia she'd had to

28

sort out problems caused by his mischief making. She shuddered as she thought of his gleaming red eyes, his black greasy fur and haughty expression.

"Yes, King Rat!" said Lila. "After the christening King Tristan ordered all of the spinning wheels to be destroyed. Everyone did as he asked because no one wanted Aurelia to hurt herself. The only person who refused was King Rat. Because he can do such strong magic no one could get his spinning wheel off him. Yesterday, on Aurelia's birthday, a present arrived. Here, let me use my magic to show you what happened..."

Lila waved her wand and touched the ground. A lilac mist appeared and in the

centre of it Delphie could see a picture.
Princess Aurelia was in the garden of the
palace, wearing a beautiful pink dress. She
was dancing lightly and joyfully, turning
pirouette after pirouette, her brown hair flying
out behind her. The King and Queen were
smiling fondly and there were lots of other

guests, courtiers and servants around too.
Delphie's great friend Sugar was standing
to the side watching the princess with a
large smile on her face. There was also a
large pile of brightly wrapped presents on a

table. Princess Aurelia started to unwrap a large present and a spinning wheel with a sharp metal spindle and a rat engraved on the handle was revealed. Looking surprised and curious, Princess Aurelia bent down to look at it more closely. Delphie saw King Tristan shout and Queen Isabella rush

forward with Sugar, but it was too late. Princess Aurelia had already pricked her finger. She cried out and spun round before falling on the floor fast asleep!

Delphie caught her breath as she saw

everyone gather around the princess.
Queen Isabella began to cry and King
Tristan lifted Aurelia's sleeping body up.

"That's awful!" cried Delphie. "I can't
believe King Rat could be so horrible!"

Lila nodded and touched the picture
with her slender wand, so that it vanished.

"I did the only thing I could think of and sent everyone else in the castle to sleep too until Aurelia's prince comes and wakes her – if he ever does." She bit her lip. "He seems to have disappeared!"

"Disappeared?" Delphie echoed.

Lila nodded. "He's not at his palace. So then I went to King Rat's castle to see if he knew anything about it but it's all locked up."

'That's strange," said Delphie. She frowned. Where could the prince have gone? This really was a mystery. *There is only one thing to do*, she decided. "We should go back to King Rat's castle and see if we can find any clues," she said aloud. "At least if it's deserted we don't have to worry about bumping into him."

"OK then!" said Lila eagerly. She took Delphie's hands. "Come on! Let's go!"

The Prisoner in the Tower

Lila spun Delphie round. They twirled through the air in a cloud of silver sparkles and landed in the woods just outside King Rat's castle. The castle was built of dark stone and loomed up menacingly against the blue sky. Delphie shivered. She had been here many times before but that didn't make it any less scary.

"I'm afraid my magic can't take us any closer," said Lila apologetically. "It's not strong enough."

Delphie nodded. She knew from her past adventures that King Rat could do very powerful magic and that he could use it to stop people getting into his castle. The Sugar Plum Fairy couldn't get into King Rat's castle either.

"It really does look deserted," she said. The windows were covered with shutters and there was no sign of King Rat's mouse guards anywhere. "Let's go and explore!"

Cautiously, they set off across the grass. As they got closer to the castle, Delphie felt anxious. What if this was just a trick? She half expected King Rat's mice guards to

come pouring out of the castle. But there really did seem to be no one around.

As they reached the castle walls, she heard a faint voice. "Help! Help me!"

She looked at Lila in alarm. "Someone's in trouble!"

The calls were coming from the back of the castle.

Lila grabbed Delphie's hand. "We'd better go and see what's happening."

Quickly they made their way around the castle.

"Help!" The voice came again.

Delphie looked up at the nearby tower and gasped. A long rat's tail was hanging from one of the upstairs windows. King Rat!

King Rat's golden crown was wonky and covered with cobwebs and his purple cloak looked dusty. "You!" he exclaimed, seeing Delphie.

For a moment they both gaped at each other.

Delphie couldn't believe it. King Rat locked up in his own castle! What was going on?

King Rat broke the silence. "Well, are you just going to stand there, girl?" he said

crossly. "I've been sitting here for days and no one's come. What are you waiting for? Get me out!"

"Maybe it's a trap," Delphie whispered to Lila.

"Come on! Start rescuing me – now, now, NOW!" shouted King Rat.

Delphie frowned. "You don't deserve rescuing after what you did to Aurelia!"

"Me?" King Rat exclaimed indignantly. "That was nothing to do with me!"

"I don't believe you," Delphie said, putting her hands on her hips.

"Me neither!" said Lila.

"But it wasn't," King Rat insisted. "Look, get me down from here and I'll tell you the whole story."

But Delphie didn't trust him at all. "No. Tell us the story and then *maybe* we'll rescue you."

King Rat sighed. "OK. OK. Well, it really *wasn't* me. It was that Wicked Fairy. She came here wanting my spinning wheel but I said no. I've never liked her – she's got two cousins of mine attached to her carriage as her prisoners. They have to pull her wherever she wants to go. So I said, I wasn't going to help her and what did she go and do? She used her magic on me!" He looked really indignant. "In my own castle!"

"You're lying!" said Delphie triumphantly. "I knew it. No one can use magic on you in your castle. This *is* just a trick!"

"Oh, the Wicked Fairy can use magic all right," King Rat replied. "She's not one of these wimpy, goody-goody fairies with their sticking out tutus and silly ballet shoes." He glanced at Lila. "With that black wand of hers, the Wicked Fairy's magic is as strong as mine…"

"He's right," Lila told Delphie. "The Wicked Fairy can do lots more magic than me and Sugar."

"Anyway, as I said, before I knew it I was shut in this tower," King Rat continued. "She whisked my mouse guards away to the other side of Enchantia, took the spinning wheel and put a spell on all the doors in the castle to lock them tight. So now I'm trapped." He looked at Delphie. "But... if you rescue me I'll help you."

"Why would we need your help?" Delphie said, crossing her arms.

"Well, how are you going to find the right prince otherwise? The one that can unlock the spell?" King Rat said, flicking his whiskers rather grandly. "I know what's happened to him and where to look for him."

"The prince?" asked Delphie. "Aurelia's *true love*."

"The very one," King Rat said smugly as he preened himself.

"So, where is he?" asked Delphie.

"Aha," said King Rat. "That would be telling. But help me escape and I *will* tell you."

Lila turned to Delphie. "My magic isn't strong enough to fight the Wicked Fairy if she really is behind all this. We'd need his help. I think we should set him free."

Delphie looked at King Rat. He'd been the cause of so much mischief in the past. "But what if it's a trick?"

"A trick?" King Rat exploded. "Do you think I like it up here, girl? Do you think I

like having nothing to eat but cobwebs and no one to shout at – well, apart from you?"

Delphie hesitated. She wanted to believe him – wanted to believe that it hadn't been him causing trouble this time. Suddenly she heard Madame Za-Za's voice in her head: *Everyone deserves a chance.*

She made up her mind.

"All right, we'll rescue you," she declared.

King Rat punched the air. "Yes!"

"But you have to give us your word that you will help us in return," Delphie added quickly.

"Whatever," said King Rat swiftly. "I promise. Just get me out of here RIGHT NOW!"

"OK." Delphie looked around. The doors were all locked and the room King Rat was in was way up high, the window barred.

"Um, Delphie?" Lila whispered. "How *are* we going to get him out?"

Delphie thought for a moment. Lila's magic was their only chance. "Can you stop your spells so Lila can do strong magic out here in your grounds?" she asked King Rat.

"Yes," he said. He waved his hands and muttered a string of words. "She should be able to do her magic now."

Delphie turned to Lila. "Can you magic up a rope ladder long enough to get from the window to the ground? Then King Rat could maybe squeeze out between the bars and get down."

But to Delphie's dismay, Lila shook her head. "I can't do that type of magic. I can't make things appear like Sugar or transform things like Cinderella's fairy godmother. I can change other fairies' spells, like I did at Aurelia's christening or use my magic to give people blessings like wealth, happiness or beauty."

"Oi!" protested King Rat from up above. "I –" he preened his whiskers – "am considered rather a catch already, I'll have you know."

Delphie ignored him. "Giving him blessings isn't going to help." She frowned. "But what about changing spells? Could you change the Wicked Fairy's spell on the locks so that instead of being closed they were open?"

"Yes!" exclaimed Lila. "It would take a lot of magic but I could do it."

"You know that's not a bad plan," King Rat said, sounding astonished. "You're not quite as stupid as you look, girl."

Lila brushed down her tutu. "I'll have to dance to make the magic work though."

Delphie stood back as King Rat groaned. "Argh! No! Not dancing!"

Lila ignored him. "Will you help me, Delphie? With two of us dancing the magic

should be stronger and it'll be easier to change the spell."

"Of course I'll help!" said Delphie eagerly. She always loved to dance. "What do you want me to do?"

Lila smiled. "Watch me first and then have a go!" She raised both arms above her head, and stood gracefully on her pointes. Then she waved her slender silver wand in a circle and music – a grand sweeping waltz – flooded through the air. Lila crossed her

left foot behind her and pointed her right
toe forward. Sweeping her arms round she
stepped on to her right toe, lifting her
other leg high in the air behind her and
opening her arms wide. From there, she
moved into a rapid spin, stepping out of it
on to her left toe. She spun round again
before jumping forward three times. Then
she waved her wand to stop the music and
looked at Delphie.

Delphie's heart had been sinking as she
had watched the fairy. "I can't do that," she
said anxiously. "I won't be able to dance as
gracefully as you, or to get my leg that high."

Lila took her hands, her blue eyes meeting
Delphie's. "Just do it as well as you can. It
doesn't matter if it is perfect or not. As long

as you dance with your heart, the magic *will* happen."

She led Delphie to where she had started from and struck the opening pose. Heart beating fast, Delphie copied her. Lila waved her wand and the music started again. Delphie felt a moment of nerves but they vanished as the beautiful music flowed through her. She moved forward, following Lila as best she could, keeping her shoulders down, her arms open, her feet light. The music – and her shoes – seemed to guide her.

On the third time of repeating the sequence, the music grew louder and

Lila spun round in a rapid pirouette after
the jumps. She stopped in perfect balance
with her wand pointing at the castle and
said: *"The Wicked Fairy's evil spell my dance
will turn about. Locks spring open at my cry
and let the big rat out."*

There was a flash and then Delphie heard a click from the lock in the back door.

The music stopped. Delphie ran to the door and tried the handle. It turned. "The locks have opened!" she cried.

"Hooray!" yelled King Rat and he disappeared from the window.

"We did it!" Lila said, hugging Delphie.

A minute later, King Rat came charging out of the back door. "I'm free!" He grinned nastily. "And now I'm off!"

And with that he charged away towards the woods, cloak flying behind him!

The Wicked Fairy's Palace

For a moment Delphie was too surprised to move and then she raced after King Rat. "Hey!" she shouted. "Just you wait here a minute! You promised you'd help us out, and a promise is a promise!"

King Rat glanced behind him. "You really thought I'd keep my word?" he yelled as he ran. "Ha! Not a chance! I'm

out of here! I'm going to get some food and… OW!" He'd been so busy talking he didn't realise he'd reached the edge of the woods and he bumped straight into a tree.

With a yell, he bounced off it and landed at Delphie's feet. She jumped on his cloak, pinning him down.

"Let me go!" he said, struggling to get up.

"No! You promised you'd help us!" said Delphie angrily.

Lila had caught up with them. "If you don't help I'll… I'll…"

"You'll what?" demanded King Rat. "You can't do much apart from give people blessings. Well, hey! Go ahead! Make me wealthy or happy then!"

"She won't do that,"
Delphie said quickly.
"But she will make you
really beautiful." King
Rat opened his mouth
but Delphie didn't give
him a chance to speak.
"But it'll be a fairy
godmother's idea of
beauty!"

Lila's eyes sparkled.
"I think I know what you mean, Delphie.
Something like *this*!" She waved her wand
and a mist appeared. In the clouds of white
was a picture of King Rat. But it was a very
different-looking King Rat! He had long
golden blond hair, big blue eyes, his nose

turned up at the end and there was a sweet
smile on his ratty face.

"Argh!" King Rat yelled, shuffling backwards
on his bottom. "No, please no!" he said,
shaking his head and holding his paws
up. "I'll do anything! Just don't make me
look like that!"

Delphie looked at him sternly. "In that case will you help us to rescue the prince like you *promised*?"

King Rat nodded. "I'll do it! I'll do anything!"

Delphie grinned at Lila. "So where is he?"

"At the Wicked Fairy's Palace!" grimaced King Rat. "In the stable block – that's where he's being kept captive."

Delphie smiled. "Then I think we'd better all go there!" she said. "Immediately!"

Lila's magic set them down behind a large bush, just outside a grey castle that was somehow more menacing than King Rat's. Tall pointed turrets reached into the sky

and black flags, each with the picture
of a green toad, flew from them. The roof
was jagged and made Delphie think of
crocodile teeth.

A shiver ran down her spine; what must
the Wicked Fairy be like?

"That's where she's keeping the prince,"

King Rat said, pointing to a stone stable block next to the castle. Five of the six doors were bolted shut.

Just then there was the sound of wheels coming down the drive. They all ducked behind the bush as a dusty black carriage appeared. It was pulled by two giant black rats galloping along on all fours and a large fairy with grey hair and warts was driving

them, hitting the reins down on their backs. "Go faster!" she shrieked at the poor rats. "Faster!"

"The Wicked Fairy!" Delphie breathed.

The fairy was wearing a swirling black dress with a full skirt and a floor-length green cloak and she had a long black wand in her hand. "STOP!" she yelled, yanking on the reins.

"They're my cousins," hissed King Rat.
"The ones I told you about. They can't
escape. She's used her magic to attach their
tails to the carriage."

Delphie saw that the ends of the rats'
tails were wound around the bar at the
front of the carriage. "But that's horrible!"
she said, as the two giant rats collapsed,
exhausted, on the ground.

There was the sound of shouting and fists
banging against a door in the stables. The
prince had obviously heard the Wicked
Fairy arrive.

"Oh, be quiet, you!" snarled the Wicked
Fairy. "And don't *you* be so lazy!" she
snapped, kicking one of the rats. "Good for
nothing, idle layabouts." She lifted her foot

with its high-heeled shoe to stamp on the other rat's paw.

Delphie couldn't bear it. She leaped out from behind the bush. "Stop it!" she shouted furiously. "Stop treating them like that!"

The Wicked Fairy swung round. "Who are you?" Her eyes fell on Delphie's red ballet shoes. "Hmm... You're that meddling human girl I've heard about. Here to try and free the prince no doubt. Well, we'll soon see about that! Prepare to turn into a statue!" She raised her wand: *"From flesh to stone you will turn. And so a lesson you will learn!"*

"No!" Lila shrieked as a bolt of green magic shot out of the Wicked Fairy's wand and headed straight for Delphie!

Saved!

Before the curse could reach Delphie, King Rat thrust his paw out. A red ball flew from his claws, colliding with the Wicked Fairy's green magic and exploding in a harmless shower of sparks.

Delphie swung round. "King Rat, you saved me!" she gasped.

"Why you... you...." The Wicked Fairy

looked like she was about to explode.
"You'll be sorry for that, King Rat," she
snarled. She waved her
wand. "You'll *all*
be sorry!"

They backed
away.

The Wicked Fairy
advanced on King
Rat. "You first. You
can join your
useless cousins and
pull my carriage!"

"No!" exclaimed King Rat.

"Yes. You won't be able to stop this
spell," she cried. "I'll use my strongest
magic and you'll be my servant forever!

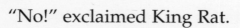

That'll serve you right for standing against me!"

Delphie looked round desperately. King Rat had helped her and now she wanted to help him but what could she do?

The Wicked Fairy cackled. "Oh, I'm going to enjoy this!"

Delphie's thoughts raced. Lila wouldn't be able to stop the spell. Their only hope was to distract the Wicked Fairy in some way. But how? An idea began to form in her brain. "Lila!" she whispered while the fairy's attention was on King Rat. "Can you change the curse on the rats so they're attached to the Wicked Fairy? Then she'll be so busy trying to free herself that she won't have time to cast the spell on King Rat."

Lila nodded. "Yes but I'll need your help again."

"Let's do it!" said Delphie.

Lila waved her wand in a very small circle and faint music flooded out.

Delphie and Lila began the dance they had done earlier.

The Wicked Fairy swung round. "What are you doing?" she demanded, as they spun and turned. "What are..."

But she was too late. Lila was already stopping, one leg held behind her, arms outstretched. *"Your curse on the rats, I will now change and twist. Tails wound not around a carriage, but around your wrists!"* She pointed her wand at the Wicked Fairy.

There was a lilac flash and suddenly the

two rats' tails were wrapped round the
Wicked Fairy's wrists. The rats leaped
forward and the Wicked Fairy bumped
down on to her large bottom.

"Ow! Eee! Ow! STOP!" she shouted in
shock as they pulled her along the ground.

"Good spell!" King Rat exclaimed.

Delphie couldn't help giggling. The Wicked Fairy looked so funny being towed along!

"She'll break the spell on the rats and free them!" Lila said, breathless with excitement.

She was right. The Wicked Fairy waved her wand. *The curse on these two rats now be broken. Set them free; my will I've spoken!* she screeched.

The two rats' tails unwound in an instant and the Wicked Fairy jolted to a stop. But as she did so, she lost her grip on her wand. It clattered to the ground.

Lila grabbed it. At the same moment, King Rat drew his sword and charged at the Wicked Fairy. "You'd treat my relatives

like that, would you?" he yelled, his red eyes gleaming. "Just wait till I get my paws on you!"

The Wicked Fairy jumped to her feet and raced to the nearest place –the open stable. She ran inside it, pulling the door shut behind her.

King Rat slammed the bolts across. "Ha!" he yelled. "Now, see how *you* like being locked up!"

Delphie and Lila hugged each other in delight.

"I'm going to see if my cousins are all right," said King Rat and he set off to comfort his relatives.

"How are we going to keep her in there?" said Delphie, expecting the Wicked Fairy to burst out at any moment.

"It's OK. She can't get out," Lila said. "Fairy magic in Enchantia comes from our wands and from dancing. The Wicked Fairy has never been able to dance and now she doesn't have her wand either, so she can't magic her way out of the stable! King Rat was right. She really *is* trapped in there!"

Delphie breathed a sigh of relief. She

couldn't help thinking that it was a deserving punishment.

"I'll come back and let her out later," Lila promised as the Wicked Fairy screeched and kicked the stable door. "But first we need to help Aurelia, and that means taking her true prince to her."

Delphie and Lila ran to let the prince out. He was very dirty, very dishevelled and very confused.

"What's been going on?" he asked.

Delphie and Lila quickly told him what had been happening. "So we need you to come with us and break the spell," said Lila.

"Of course," said the prince, sweeping into a graceful bow. "It would be an honour. Prince Florimund at your service."

"There's no time for that flowery nonsense," said Lila impatiently. "Princess Aurelia needs us. Let's go!"

King Rat came over just in time to overhear. "The job's done then here," he said. "You've got your prince and the Wicked Fairy's locked up."

"Thank you so much for helping us,"
Delphie smiled at him.

"Humph!" said King Rat. But he looked
secretly pleased. He cleared his throat.
"Well, I'm off now. My cousins have invited
me back to their mansion for a slap-up
meal." He rubbed his stomach. "No more
cobwebs for me!"

"But aren't you going to come and see
Princess Aurelia waking up?" asked
Delphie in surprise.

"Hmmm." King Rat looked suspicious.
"Everyone will be really happy when that
happens, won't they?"

"Of course," said Delphie.

"So, there'll be…" A shudder ran through
King Rat. *"Dancing?"*

Lila grinned. "Oh yes, there'll be dancing."

"Urgh!" said King Rat. And he stomped quickly off. "Dancing, dancing, all they ever think about is dancing. If I had my way I'd stop it all…"

Delphie grinned to herself. King Rat might have turned out to be unusually nice this time but some things *never* changed.

Hearing the sound of music behind her, she turned. Lila had joined the prince and was waving her wand. "Come on, we must get Prince Florimund to the palace."

Delphie ran to join them and in a whirl of sparkles Lila whisked them away.

Back at the Palace

Lila's magic took them straight to Aurelia's bedroom. The princess was curled up in a pink dress on her big bed, sleeping peacefully. Queen Isabella was asleep beside her and King Tristan was at the end of the bed. Looking out of the window at the courtyard below, Delphie could see that all the servants and courtiers were also asleep.

"She's so beautiful," Prince Florimund said in an awed voice.

"Kiss her," Lila urged. "Break the spell!"

The handsome young prince approached the bed. He bent down and kissed Aurelia gently.

Delphie held her breath. What if he couldn't break the spell?

The princess stirred and blinked. She stared at Prince Florimund. Her blue eyes widened and she smiled. "Who are you?" she breathed.

"Your prince," he replied softly.

Delphie and Lila exchanged delighted looks as he hugged Princess Aurelia. The King and Queen both started to wake up. Hearing noises from outside, Delphie ran to the window. The servants and courtiers were shaking their heads, rubbing their eyes, stretching and yawning.

"Everyone's waking up!" she said. "The curse is broken!"

Aurelia got to her feet. She had been whispering to the prince.

Holding her hand, he got down on one knee. "Will you marry me, Aurelia?" he said.

Princess Aurelia smiled. "I will."

The Queen gasped. "You're getting married!"

"Yes, Mother," Aurelia cried as Prince Florimund stood up and swung her round. "I am!"

Everyone in the palace turned out to celebrate. King Tristan and Queen Isabella were so delighted that they organised a betrothal banquet and soon the musicians were playing and platters of food were being put down on the tables.

"Oh, Delphie," said Princess Aurelia. "I'm so happy! Thank you so much for bringing Prince Florimund to me."

"You saved the day again," said Sugar, appearing at Delphie's side, yawning after her long sleep.

Delphie and Lila had told everyone about their adventures.

"I can't believe King Rat actually helped!" Princess Aurelia said.

"I know. And he even stopped the Wicked Fairy turning me to stone!" Delphie said.

"I suppose that means I'll have to invite him to the wedding," Princess Aurelia grinned. "Maybe some day we'll be able to convince him that dancing is the most wonderful thing in the world! Come on, everyone," she called. "Let's dance!"

Lila and Delphie ran on to the floor with everyone else and as Prince Florimund joined Aurelia, she took his hand, and the music began.

They danced round the room holding hands, their other arms stretched out gracefully at their sides. It was a fast dance with lots of light skipping with pointed toes and every so often they would change direction or stop and one person would dance lightly around the other.

Then they would all set off again. It was such fun! They swapped partners and after dancing with Lila, Delphie found herself dancing with the prince and then Princess Aurelia and then Sugar. Her head spun. It had been an amazing adventure!

Just as the dance started coming to an end, she felt her feet tingling. She knew what that meant. "I'm about to go home!" she gasped. "Bye, Princess Aurelia! Bye, Lilac and Sugar! Bye, Prince Florimund!"

"Bye, Delphie!" they called and the next moment Delphie was spinning away in a whirl of colours. She spun faster and faster until she landed on a hard floor. She blinked her eyes open and found herself outside the ballet studio, looking in at Rosa practising her *pas de chats*.

Delphie took a deep breath. She felt like she had been away ages, but in real life no time had passed. She looked at Rosa and at the same moment Rosa glanced at the door and saw her watching. The new girl looked

quickly away, her cheeks flushing.

Delphie hesitated. Her adventure had taught her that people weren't always as they seemed. Even King Rat had helped her out when she'd been in trouble. *Maybe Poppy and Lola are right and she's just shy,* thought Delphie. *That can sometimes make people say the wrong thing. But…*

Everyone deserves a chance, Delphie…

She heard Madame Za-Za's voice in her head and making up her mind, Delphie opened the ballet studio door and went inside.

Rosa

Rosa looked round and blushed.

"Hi," said Delphie. "I was wondering…"

"Delphie, I'm really sorry about yesterday in the changing room." The words stammered out of Rosa before Delphie could say any more. The new girl twisted her hands round in front of her, looking at the floor. "I should have said sorry straight away but I

was too embarrassed. I… I didn't mean to sound like you couldn't do *petit jetés*. It just came out wrong."

Delphie was taken aback. "That's OK. I…"

"I only said it because I was going to offer to help you with them," interrupted Rosa. "But you got cross and then I felt awful. You're a much better dancer than I am. Of course you're not going to want someone like me to help." She looked at the floor, as if she was wishing it would swallow her up.

Delphie felt a weight lift from her. She hurried forward. "Don't be silly, Rosa. And actually you *are* better than me at *petit jetés*, so it was really nice of you to offer to help.

I'm sorry I got cross."

Rosa lifted her eyes from the floor. She looked as if she couldn't quite believe it.

"Why don't we help each other?" Delphie suggested.

"I was watching you and I think you're getting the *pas de chats* wrong because you're jumping off the front foot. What you need to do is keep your knees out more and start from the back foot, like this." She showed Rosa what she meant, jumping lightly to one side. "You

try now. Imagine you're leaping over a gate."

With Delphie helping and encouraging her, Rosa soon managed to do the step much better.

"Now will you help me?" asked Delphie. "Show me what *I'm* doing wrong."

They practised together until Delphie began to get it right.

"That's loads better!" she said, enjoying the feeling of doing it properly. She glanced at the clock on the wall. There was still some time until the lesson began. "Should we just do some dancing?" she said. "I learned this dance recently. It's from *Sleeping Beauty*. I could show you how to do it. It's really good fun!"

"Oh, yes please!" said Rosa.

Delphie soon taught Rosa the basic skipping step and the way of turning and changing direction. Rosa was a natural dancer who picked up things very quickly.

Delphie went over to the CD player where there was a shelf of CDs. "Let's do it to music!" She found the CD of *Sleeping Beauty* and put on the track. Soon, she and

Rosa were dancing around the room, skipping and spinning, spinning and dancing. Doing some steps properly but making up others and letting the music speak to them. It was a brilliant feeling to be dancing so freely.

They stopped, both out of breath. Rosa's eyes were sparkling. "That was fantastic!"

"It was," agreed Delphie happily.

A movement at the studio door caught her eyes. Madame Za-Za was watching them. Delphie's eyes flew to hers. *Everyone deserves a chance*, she thought.

And Madame Za-Za smiled.

Darcey's Magical Masterclass

Sleeping Beauty Awakes

Here's a fun dance which shows the waking of Princess Aurelia from the wicked spell.

1.
Start with your arms and head down, as if you are asleep.

2.
Slowly raise up your arms and head, stretching right up into the air.

3.
Sweep your
arms back
down and
gently rub your
eyes to wake
yourself up!

4.
Spin round in
a circle
holding your
arms out.

*Magic
Ballerina*™
Delphie and the Birthday Show

Delphie's friends in Enchantia need her
help again! Can Delphie reverse a horrible
spell cast by King Rat and save the
Queen's special Birthday show?

**Read on for a sneak preview
of book six…**

ஃ・٭・☆・ஃ・☆・٭・☆・٭・ஃ

Delphie heard the sound of shouting from inside the palace and someone came running out. Her heart leaped. It was the Sugar Plum Fairy!

Delphie was about to call out when she saw Prince Florimund running out of the palace after Sugar.

"Sugar, wait! I love you!" he said, throwing himself at her feet.

"Florimund!" Sugar cried crossly, pushing him away. "Stop this! I don't love you and you don't love me. You love Aurelia!"

With that, she spun round with her arms above her head, and vanished.

"She's gone!" Prince Florimund cried despairingly. And lying on the ground he burst into tears.

Delphie stared in astonishment. *What was going on?*

Then the palace door flew open and Aurelia came running out, her face pale. "Florimund!"

"No, Aurelia!" Prince Florimund said, scrambling to his feet. "I do not love you!"

"Aurelia!" Delphie raced over to her friend. "What's happening?"

"Oh, Delphie! Thank goodness you're here! Please can you help me? Please!"

°ⓞ˙*˙☆˙ⓞ˙*˙☆˙ⓞ˙*˙☆˙ⓞ˙*˙°

Magic Ballerina

Darcey Bussell

Buy more great Magic Ballerina books direct from HarperCollins
at **10%** off recommended retail price.
FREE postage and packing in the UK.

Delphie and the Magic Ballet Shoes	ISBN 978 0 00 728607 2
Delphie and the Magic Spell	ISBN 978 0 00 728608 9
Delphie and the Masked Ball	ISBN 978 0 00 728610 2
Delphie and the Glass Slippers	ISBN 978 0 00 728617 1
Delphie and the Fairy Godmother	ISBN 978 0 00 728611 9
Delphie and the Birthday Show	ISBN 978 0 00 728612 6

All priced at £3.99

To purchase by Visa/Mastercard/Switch simply call
08707871724 or fax on **08707871725**

To pay by cheque, send a copy of this form with a cheque made payable to
'HarperCollins Publishers' to: Mail Order Dept. (Ref: BOB4),
HarperCollins Publishers, Westerhill Road, Bishopbriggs, G64 2QT,
making sure to include your full name, postal address and phone number.

From time to time HarperCollins may wish to use your personal data
to send you details of other HarperCollins publications and offers.
If you wish to receive information on other HarperCollins publications
and offers please tick this box ☐

Do not send cash or currency. Prices correct at time of press.
Prices and availability are subject to change without notice.
Delivery overseas and to Ireland incurs a £2 per book postage and packing charge.